BRIDGET FIDGET

Joe Berger

PUFFIN

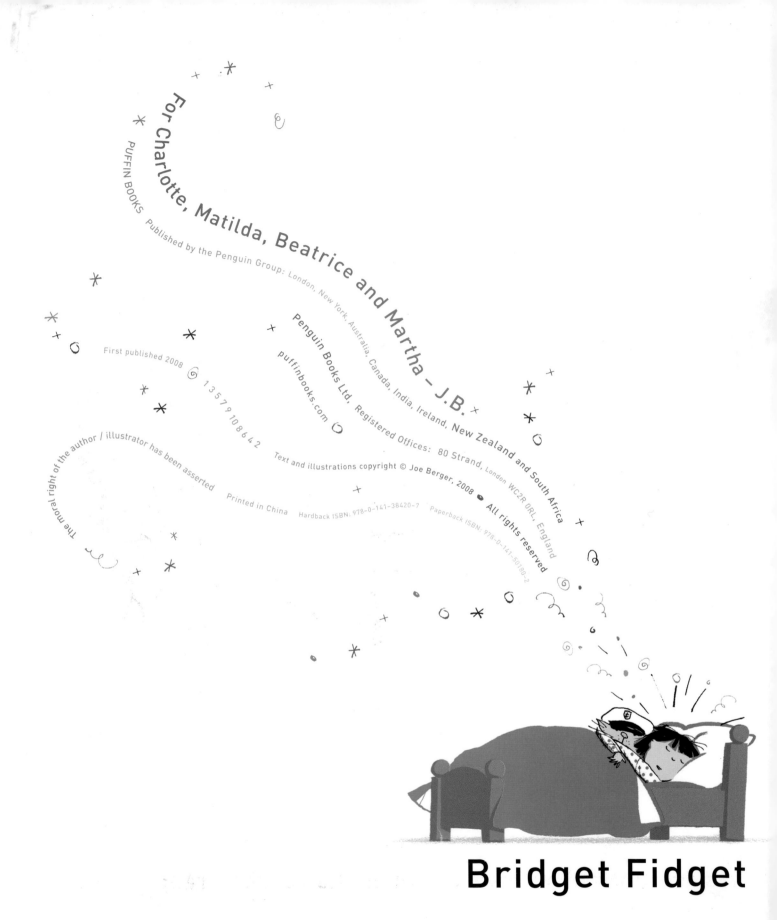

For Charlotte, Matilda, Beatrice and Martha – J.B.

PUFFIN BOOKS

Published by the Penguin Group: London, New York, Australia, Canada, India, Ireland, New Zealand and South Africa

Penguin Books Ltd, Registered Offices: 80 Strand, London WC2R 0RL, England

puffinbooks.com

First published 2008

1 3 5 7 9 10 8 6 4 2

Text and illustrations copyright © Joe Berger, 2008

The moral right of the author / illustrator has been asserted

Printed in China

Hardback ISBN: 978-0-141-38420-7   Paperback ISBN: 978-0-141-50180-2

Bridget Fidget

was dreaming about pets . . . when the doorbell rang.

She **leapt** out of bed,

put her clothes on
and *raced* downstairs
with Captain Cat.

But when Bridget got downstairs,
all she found was a **great big box**.

It was decorated with lovely ribbons
that probably said *"Congratulations!"*
and *"Here's your new pet!"*
or something like that.

It's a bit small
for a unicorn.

And it was filled
with all sorts of snow.

Maybe
it's a penguin,
Captain Cat!

This box wouldn't open.
Bridget sniffed it.
It didn't **smell**.

Bridget **shook** it.
It didn't squeak.

Bridget *rolled* it.
It didn't skitter.

Maybe it's
NOT a mouse.

Just then, the box began to make a noise.

It's asleep, Captain Cat! There's a sleepy little secret pet in the box and we need to WAKE IT UP!

A shower is good for waking up.

But Daddy was already
in the shower.

Then again . . .
if we wake it up
too soon, it might
be grumpy.

So Bridget tucked the box up in bed with Mummy.

Sssshhhhhh!

Daddy didn't like the snow one bit.

He made a **LOT** of noise,
which woke up Mummy.

Luckily, Daddy cheered up
when he saw the box.

Bridget couldn't help feeling *a little* disappointed.

But then, the noise started again.

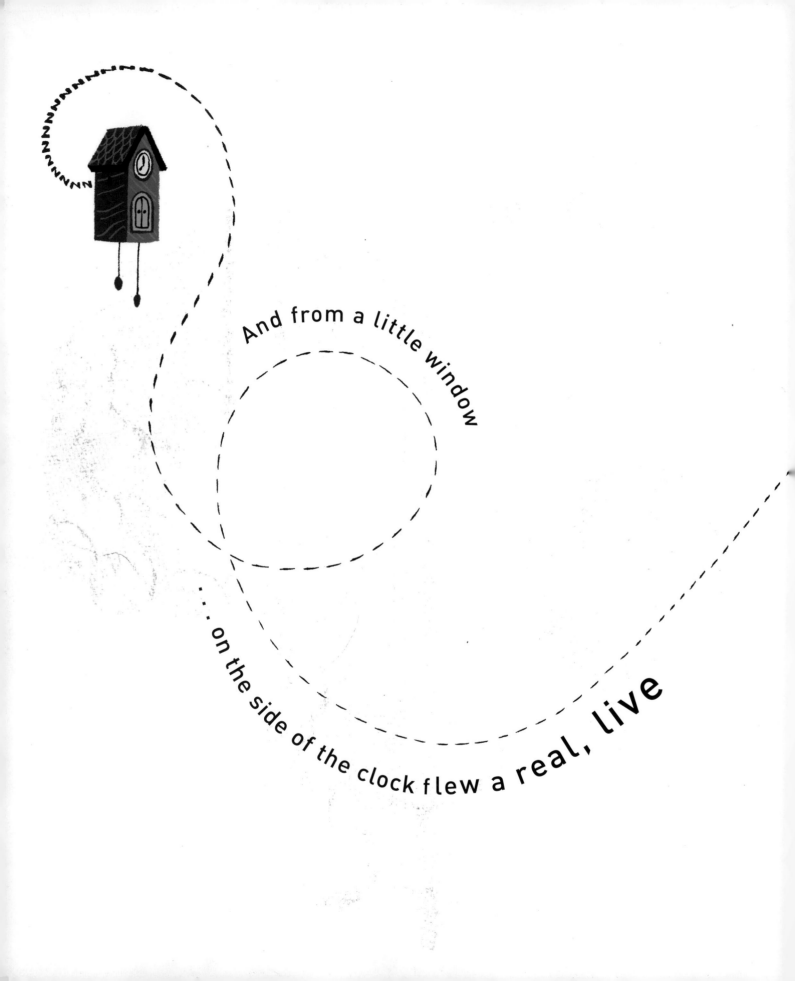

And from a little window

... on the side of the clock flew **a real, live**

A ladybird that was
much less **skittery**
than a pet mouse

and could
fly much **higher**
than a pet penguin!

And as for its dancing . . .

Easily as good as a pet unicorn!

Bridget called her ladybird **Thunderhooves**

. . . the best little surprise pet in the world!